Mr Smudge's Thirsty Day

Jonathan Gunson

Ashton Scholastic

Auckland   Sydney   New York   Toronto   Lo⌐

*Mr Smudge is a Siamese cat
who likes his bowl of
fresh water each day.
When he finds it empty,
he goes looking for a drink
and has all sorts of
surprising adventures!*

For James

First published in hardback by Reed Methuen Publishers Ltd
as a Dorothy Butler Book, 1985.
This paperback edition published by Ashton Scholastic Ltd, 1989.

Ashton Scholastic Limited
Private Bag 1, Penrose, Auckland 5, New Zealand.

Ashton Scholastic Pty Ltd
P.O. Box 579, Gosford, NSW 2250, Australia.

Scholastic Inc.
730 Broadway, New York, NY 10003, USA.

Scholastic-TAB Publications Ltd
123 Newkirk Road, Richmond Hill, Ontario L4C 3G5, Canada.

Scholastic Publications Ltd
Marlborough House, Holly Walk, Leamington Spa, Warwickshire CV32 4LS,
England.

Copyright © Jonathan Gunson, 1985

National Library of New Zealand
Cataloguing-in-Publication data

Gunson, Jonathan.
   Mr Smudge's thirsty day/Jonathan Gunson.
Auckland, N.Z.: Ashton Scholastic, 1989.
   1 v.
   Children's picture story book.
   First published: Auckland (N.Z.): Reed Methuen,
1985.
   ISBN 1-86943-019-0
   I.Title
   NZ823.2

54321   9/8   0123/9
Printed in Hong Kong

Mr Smudge always had a bowl of
cool water to drink.
One day, the family forgot to give him one.

Mr Smudge was soon
thirsty so off he went
to find something
to drink.

He liked the drips from the kitchen tap,
but his tongue got tired.

And the wash tub water was
full of soap bubbles.

He found a big round glass bowl of water,
but it had a fish swimming in it.
This made Mr Smudge hungry
as well as thirsty,
but the cover stayed firmly in place.

So he strolled into
the garden
to look a little further.

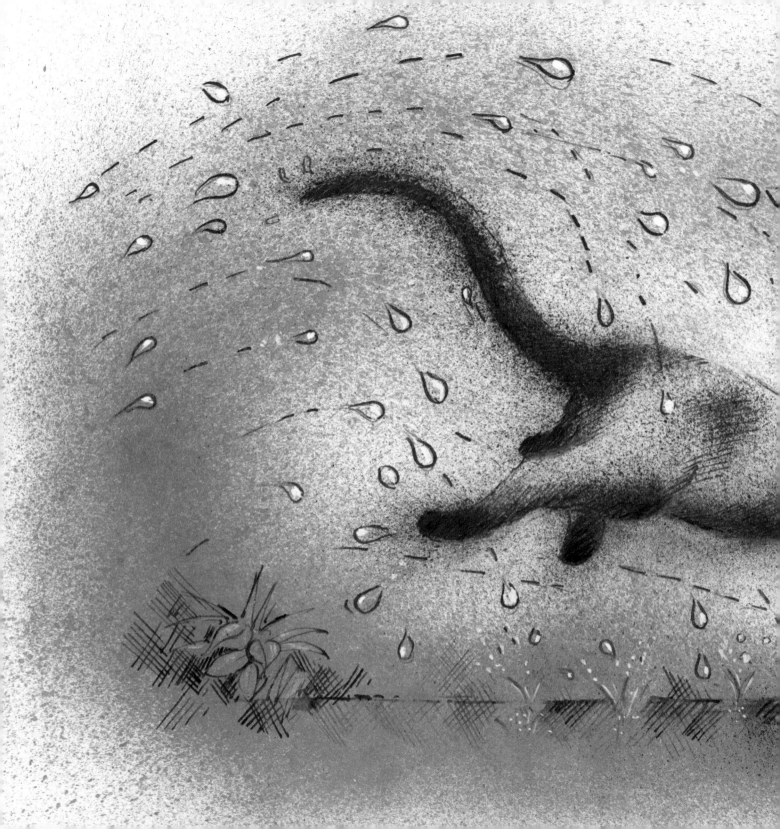

He saw a sprinkler and jumped
to catch the drops
but his fur got wet.

A watering can tipped over with a crash and a splash when he tried to drink from it.

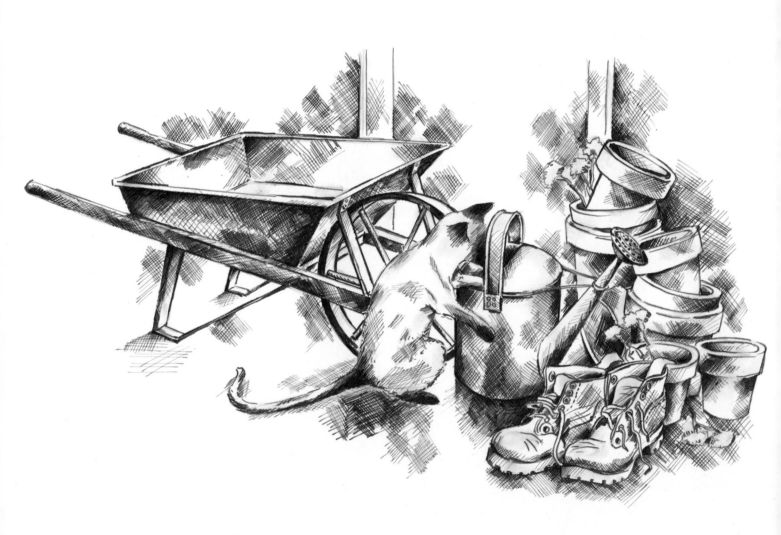

This made Mr Smudge even
thirstier, so he slipped
through the garden fence
into the big world.

He found a cool clean
puddle,
but somebody splashed
in it with muddy boots.

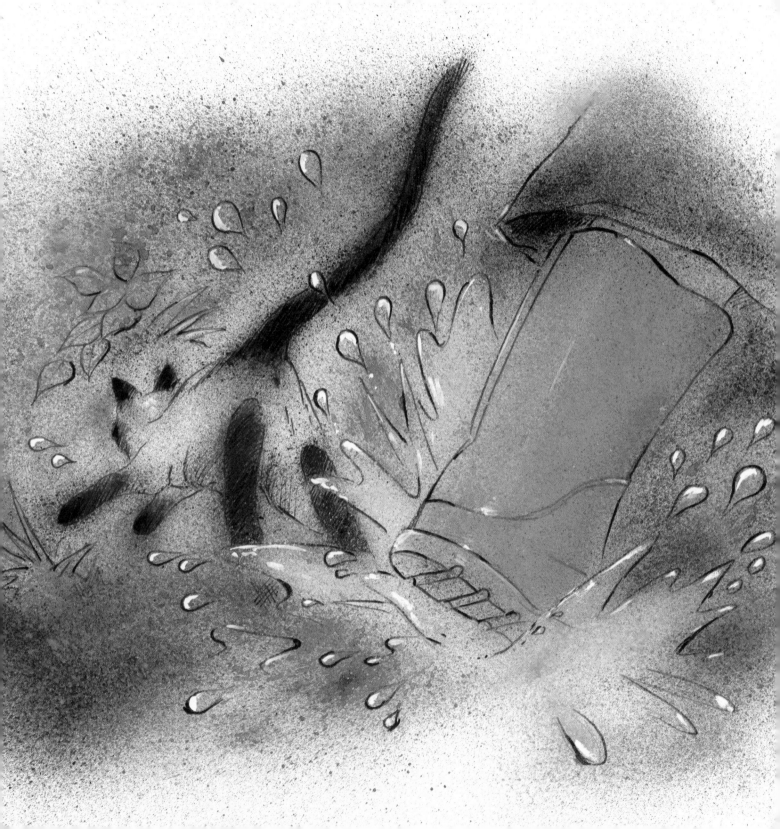

Water from a fire hose rushed at him fast.

And the sea was too salty.

Just then it began to rain
and started to grow dark.
Big drops splashed down all around.

Mr Smudge dashed back home so fast, his paws hardly touched the ground.

He leapt over the garden fence
and raced indoors.

MMMM...MM...!

What was that
lovely smell?

It was a fish dinner
all ready for him.

And what do you think
he found as well?

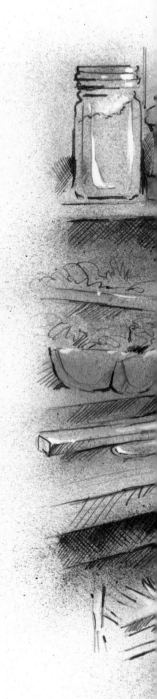

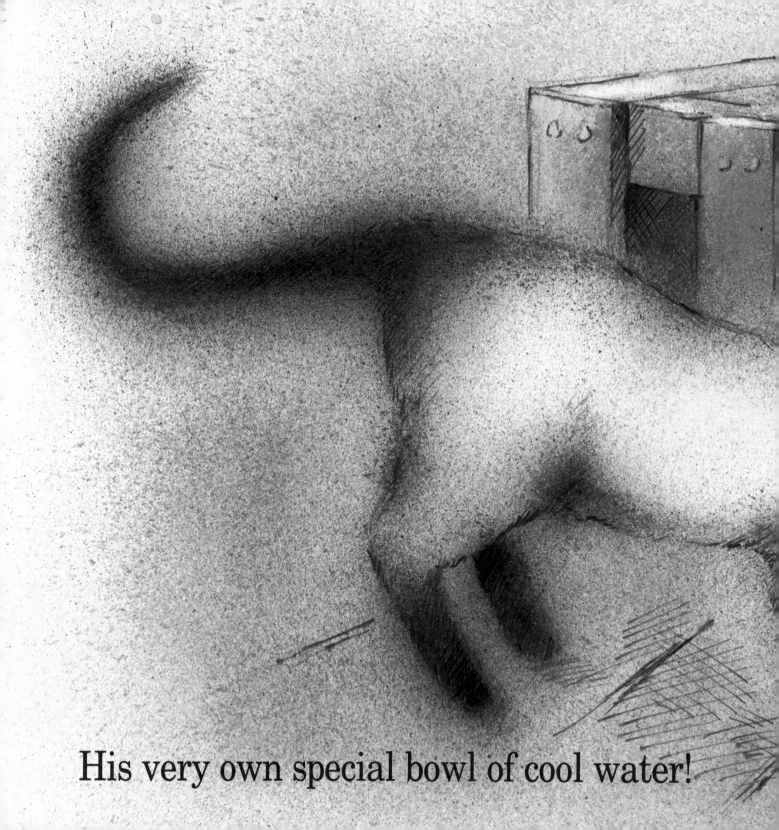

His very own special bowl of cool water!

The End.